Oh No, MonSTeR TOMATO!

For Sam
(and the **Little Apple!**),
for smiling **Joe**,
and for **Maisie**
and **George**

Oh No, MoNSTeR ToMATO!

Jim Helmore

Karen Wall

EGMONT

It was time for the
Great Grislygust Grow-off.

GROW-OFF!

Prize for
top crop

WELCOME TO
GRISLYGUST

GROW-OFF!

Prize for
top crop

GROW-OFF!

Prize for
top crop

This year Marvin
planned to grow
the tastiest tomatoes
in town.

But his beastly brother, Boris, and
his poisonous sister, Prunella,
had other ideas.

"You're a titchy weed, Marvin," they bellowed.

"And your tomatoes will be tiny too!"

"I'll show **them**," thought Marvin.

He studied his gardening books carefully.

HANCOCKS HORTICULTURAL HORRORS

Keep Out!

His tomato plant
would be . . .

. . . something
very special.

The people of Grislygust . . .

pruned . . .

and polished . . .

. . . and pampered their vegetables.

Boris's beans **curled** up their canes . . .

and Prunella's pumpkins were **plumping up** nicely.

But there was no sign of Marvin's tomatoes.

"Your tomato plant is just like you," Boris laughed. "It's forgotten how to grow!"

Marvin went back to his gardening books . . .

Perhaps what he needed was a special song?
Marvin took a deep breath
and began to sing:

Grow, grow, grow, Mon-ster To-ma-to!

Up, up, up, in - to the sky.

Grow, grow, grow, Mon-ster To-ma-to!

Up, up, up, so high, high, high!

The garden fell silent. There wasn't so much as the **squelch** of a slug.

Then the ground began to **GRUMBLE,**

and the soil began to **SHAKE!**

A great shoot
BURST
through the earth.

MIAOOOOOW!

SPLAT!

It hit the neighbour's cat.

"Ha–hah!!" Marvin cried.

"I've invented a new kind of fruity – shooty tomato!"

"What's going on?"
called Boris and Prunella.

"Meet my
MAGNIFICENT
MONSTER
TOMATO
PLANT!"
said Marvin.

Boris and Prunella crept
closer
and closer . . .

WHOOMPH!

Two very large and squashy fruits shot off in their direction.

"GO, GO, GO, MONSTER TOMATO!" cried Marvin.

The tomatoes splotted Marvin's brother and sister with a great

DOUBLE SPLAT!

"Yuk!" cried Prunella.

"Disgusting!" spluttered Boris.

Marvin laughed and laughed and laughed.

But then there came a knock at the garden gate. The competition judges had arrived!

"We've come to see **Boris's** beautiful beans," called one judge.

"And **Prunella's** perfect pumpkins," said another.

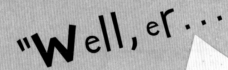

"**W**ell, er . . . could you come back later?" asked Marvin.

But the judges pushed past him.

"What in Grislygust is **THAT?**" they asked.

"NO, NO, NO, NO, MONSTER TOMATO!" cried Marvin.

But it was too late!

"WOAH, WOAH, WOAHHH, MONSTER TOMATO!"
shouted Marvin.

But his tomato plant
was out of control!

Marvin searched frantically for a grow-reversal song. Then he sang at the top of his voice:

Marvin's monster tomato gave a great **SHUDDER**,

and then a **SHIVER** . . .

and
slowly
shrank
back to
the size
of a
normal
plant.

One by one
       the judges
wiped
       themselves down
and cleaned
       themselves up.

"Marvin,"

they announced . . .

MARVIN'S TOMATOES

SIZE 10/10

SHAPE 10/10

COLOUR 10/10

TASTE 10/10

JUDGE

JUDGE

"Those tomatoes are **delicious!** They're the **tastiest** tomatoes in town...

and smiled a crafty smile . . .